Missing Jack

LION CHILDREN'S

Rebecca Elliott

I'm pretty sure that my cat Jack...

For Jack, Humphrey, and Cheeky the dog x

Published by Lion Children's Books
an imprint of
Lion Hudson plc
Wilkinson House, Jordan Hill Road,
Oxford OX2 8DR, England
www.lionhudson.com/lionchildrens

Hardback ISBN 978 0 7459 6502 4
Paperback ISBN 978 0 7459 6578 9

First edition 2015

A catalogue record for this book is available from the British Library

Printed and bound in Malaysia, October 2014, LH18

... was THE best cat EVER.

And here's why...

Some cats are snooty
and don't come near you.

But Jack was really friendly.

He sat on Clemmie's lap to keep her warm.

Other cats are ANGRY
and SCRATCHY.

But Jack never scratched.

Even when Benjamin pulled his whiskers.

Some cats are ***boring***
and never do
anything.

But Jack

thought he was a LION.

He pounced and posed
and leaped and lounged
like he was the king of the jungle.

Then Jack got a bit old.
He was like an old furry Grandpa.

He didn't chase
mice anymore.

Instead he invited them around for tea
and told them stories about the good old days.

It was almost like he was fading away.

Then Jack died.

And I miss him.

We buried his body in the garden.

Daddy played guitar and I sang him a song.
It was about a lion sleeping in the jungle.
I think he would have liked it.

My parents
say we can get
another cat
one day.

But I don't
want another cat.

I want my cat. I want Jack.

But I did meet another cat today.

His name's Humphrey and
his hobbies include

climbing up EVERYTHING,

jumping off ANYTHING, and

starting fights with ANYONE
bigger than him.

He's a little furry fearless DAREDEVIL.

He's not **Jack**.

But then he's also not

snooty,

angry and scratchy,

or *boring*.

So maybe he's not THE best cat EVER.
But he's still pretty AWESOME.

I've told Humphrey that I still miss Jack
but if he needs a place to stay, he can live here.

He seems OK with that.

Z Z Z Z

And I think Jack's OK with that too.
Z Z z